To Poppy Dave,

Thank you for always sharing your passion, and showing me that cooking isn't just about recipes and ingredients—it's about the people you share your creations with. Thank you for sparking our creative sides and allowing us to cover your kitchen with flour, all for the LOVE OF PIZZA and family.

Hey there fellow adventurers!

This is Mimi and her family. They are on a trip to New York City!

There is so much to see… and eat there!

Today they visited Grand Central Station, and Mimi now knows why they call it grand! The conductor told her that 750,000 people pass through Grand Central every day! Can you believe it?!

From the biggest train station to the smallest restaurant, pretzels and hot dogs are right there on the street! What more could Mimi ask for?

Salty… soft… pretzel goodness!

After their snack break, the family went 102 stories high to see the whole city from above!

"I can see everything from up here! It's like I am a superhero watching over the city!" said Danny.

"This is the Empire State building, of course you can see everything from up here!" said Mimi.

Next up, they took a boat ride and saw the Statue of Liberty! Did you know she was a gift from the French? She sure is big, and they say it took nine years to build Lady Liberty.

Mimi wondered if she liked pizza, too.

"How about we go to a museum next?" asked Mimi's mom.

"I think it would be way more fun if we went and got some

pizza!
Pizza!
Pizza!
Pizza!"

Mimi chanted.

"That does sound good Mimi, but let's go to the museum first and then go get pizza," said Mimi's dad.

Turns out the museum thing was really cool! "That was one of my favorite stops of the day… until we go get pizza of course!" Mimi said.

Mimi saw life size dinosaurs, giant whales, dug for fossils, and went to the planetarium! It was like being in outer space! *I wonder if they have pizza in outer space… I sure hope so!* Mimi thought.

"Look, the park! Please Mom, can we go into Central Park. It's right there!" questioned Danny.

"Mom, pizza remember? We said we were going to go get pizza! Please Mom!" begged Mimi.

"How about Danny and I go into the park, and you and Mom can go visit Uncle Joe at the pizzeria. Grab a pie and we can have a pizza picnic!" said Mimi's dad.

"Perfect idea!" shouted Mimi.

"See you later, alligators!

Mmmmm… Can you smell the pizza Mom?"

"Mimi! You made it! How are you liking New York City? So much to see, so little time! You guys must be starving. Piece of pizza anyone?" asked Uncle Joe.

"Yes! Yes! Yes! I have been waiting for pizza all day!" exclaimed Mimi.

Mimi couldn't believe her eyes. Pizza dough was everywhere: being rolled on the table, being thrown in the air, being topped with sauce!

"Uncle Joe, what makes pizza dough so special? How do you get it to taste so good?" asked Mimi.

"Well Mimi, there are so many things that make pizza so great. The dough, the sauce, the cheese, and of course the toppings.

Have you ever made pizza before Mimi?"

"No, but I have eaten A LOT!"

"Now Mimi, the dough is the most crucial part and takes the most amount of time and love to make right."

"Well luckily I love pizza, I love baking, and I have plenty of time, so I should be able to make a great dough!" said Mimi.

"We're going to put our pizza on a special baking pan called a pizza stone. Pizza bakers like to use them to get their crust nice and crispy. We are going to put it in our oven and set the temperature to 500 degrees Fahrenheit."

"Whoa! 500 degrees! That's way too hot. Everything is going to burn!" exclaimed Mimi.

"One of the secrets to having the best pizza is a very hot oven with a very hot stone to bake on," explained Uncle Joe.

"Ooey gooey cheese pizza here I come!"

"Mimi, do you know what yeast is?" asked Uncle Joe.

"Yeast? What's that?"

"Well, it's a single cell living organism that is part of the fungi family, but right now they are all sleeping. We need to wake them up so they can help make our dough rise!"

"That's alive!? And we are going to feed it? And then bake it?!"

"Just like you, yeast needs to eat to get lots of energy and grow. Yeast loves sugar and a warm environment. From there our yeast is going to come alive and start breathing its air bubbles, which will make our pizza dough rise."

Mimi and Uncle Joe mixed 1 cup of warm water, 3 teaspoons of sugar, and ¾ teaspoon of yeast in a bowl and waited for the bubbles to start!

"Sugar is all yeast gets to eat? Wow! That's some lucky yeast!" joked Mimi.

"While the yeast takes its time eating all that sugar, can you measure out 1 cup of bread flour and 1 cup of all-purpose flour, Mimi?"

"Certainly!"

Mimi scooped and swept each cup of flour and set them aside for later.

"Uncle Joe, these flours look awfully similar. Why is one called *bread flour* and the other *all-purpose*?"

"You see Mimi, bread flour has a higher amount of protein in it which will help us develop more gluten for a stronger dough. It's essential for the perfect pizza dough. There are different types of flours that work best for all different types of recipes. It all depends on what you're making! Next up on the recipe is the salt and extra virgin olive oil," said Uncle Joe.

Mimi measured her 3 tablespoons of oil and poured them into a small bowl for later. She then measured 2 teaspoons of salt and added it to her flour mixture.

"Great job, Mimi! Now that we have all our ingredients set aside, let's see if our yeast is done eating."

"Do you see that, Mimi? Look at all the bubbles that are forming. Your yeast is nice and happy!"

"It kind of smells," said Mimi.

"That's the gas that the yeast is releasing.
It's almost like the yeast is burping.

All right, now for the fun part! Let's roll up your sleeves and
get you ready for the dirty part of this job," said Uncle Joe.

Uncle Joe added the flour, salt, and oil to the yeast mixture.

Mimi wasted no time using her hands to mix and form her ingredients into a ball.

"We need to knead and work the dough for three minutes. This will help build up the gluten so it's nice and strong and can hold all of our toppings!"

Mimi worked the dough, trying to mimic the pizza makers beside her by punching, kneading, and folding the dough.

"Has it been three minutes yet? This dough is making me tired!" exclaimed Mimi.

"Two more minutes to go, Mimi!"

Mimi continued to work her dough with all her might.

"Now we need to let your dough rest in a greased bowl, covered by a dish towel to keep it nice and warm."

"Why would we do that Uncle Joe?"

"Well Mimi, your dough is tired and needs rest just like you. We are going to wait fifteen minutes, and then knead the dough again for three minutes."

"Again!? Sheesh, that dough is demanding!" laughed Mimi.

"Once we knead it again, we can allow it to rest covered in a warm environment for thirty minutes or until it doubles in size," explained Uncle Joe.

"Doubles in size? Wow that's some active yeast!"

While the dough rested, Mimi began to make her sauce for the pizza. As Uncle Joe got the blender, Mimi read the recipe and pulled together four fresh tomatoes, four leaves of basil, and three leaves of fresh oregano.

"Mmmmm… these smell so good!" exclaimed Mimi.

"Fresh ingredients make all the difference, Mimi!" said Uncle Joe.

Mimi continued with one clove of garlic, and then measured out 2 tablespoons of tomato paste.

They placed all of their ingredients into the blender. Mimi added two pinches of salt, followed by two pinches of ground black pepper.

"Ready to go, Mimi? Go ahead and press the button and let's make some sauce!"

Mimi secured the top and started the blender. She watched as her picked ingredients became the perfect tomato sauce for her pizza!

"Looks great, Mimi! Good job following the recipe. We can set that aside for later and check on our dough."

Pepper

"Uncle Joe! Uncle Joe! I think our dough is ready! It's ginormous!
Wow!" said Mimi with amazement.

They sprinkled flour on the surface of the table and placed the finished dough in the center. Mimi began to flatten her dough using the palms of her hands going around in a circle to keep that perfect pizza shape. She turned and flattened. Turned and flattened… all while keeping a ring around the outside for her crust.

"Uncle Joe, can you teach me how to throw the pizza in the air like they're doing? Mom says I shouldn't play with my food, but that sure does look like fun!"

"Actually Mimi, they do that to stretch out the dough to make it nice and thin. What you're going to do is slide your hands under the dough and create two open fists. Now slowly raise your open fists up off the table and begin to lightly toss your dough in a circular motion into the air.

Try and catch the flying dough with the back of your open fists, and continue to toss! Remember we don't want to use our fingertips to catch it because that's how it can rip."

"Look, Uncle Joe I'm doing it!"

Mimi began to toss her dough higher, and higher....

"Oh no!"

Uncle Joe quickly grabbed her dough
and brushed the flour off her face.

"Oh Mimi, practice makes perfect!" Uncle Joe chuckled.

Mimi formed her tossed dough into a circle and was ready to start topping it!

Mimi watched the pizza bakers carefully as they spread the sauce in a perfect circular swirling motion. Mimi copied as she poured a ladle of sauce in the middle of her dough. She slowly started drawing circles in the sauce with the back of her ladle, gradually making bigger and bigger circles until her whole dough was covered in sauce.

"Now the fun part, Mimi! The cheese!"

Mimi placed some chopped basil leaves on her sauce and sprinkled shredded mozzarella cheese all over her dough until it was perfectly covered.

"Here at the pizzeria, we like to use what we call a pizza peel to move the pizza in and out of the oven safely. Now remember Mimi, the oven is going to be very hot and so will the pizza stone. Always allow an adult to put your pizza in and out of the oven. Seeing that you won't have a pizza peel at home, we are going to place your dough onto parchment paper before we top it so we can easily get your pizza in and out of the oven."

Uncle Joe gently lifted the parchment paper and transferred Mimi's pizza from the table to the pizza stone in the oven.

"Remember Mimi, this part is very dangerous with such a hot oven, so make sure you let an adult help you. I will need you to set me a timer for ten minutes though."

"Pizza guard reporting to duty! Ten minutes... starting... now!"

Mimi waited patiently as her pizza baked. Bubbling cheese.
Browning crust… and the smell! Oh, the smell!

BEEEEEP!

"Uncle Joe! Uncle Joe! The pizza is ready! The crust is nice and golden brown, the cheese is ooey gooey pizza goodness! Is it time for it to come out?"

"Yes it most certainly is! Good job Mimi, your pizza looks perfect!" said Uncle Joe.

Uncle Joe removed the pizza from the oven and placed it on a cutting board to cool.

"This is a very special pizza knife, it allows you to cut your
pizza into those perfect triangles."

"It looks like a wheel," Mimi said confused.

Mimi and Uncle Joe rolled the pizza cutter across the pie creating one cut straight across. They continued by criss-crossing their original cut to create four pieces, and did the same through each section to create eight perfectly portioned slices.

"And there you have it, Mimi! New York style pizza! Let's box it up
so you can take it to Central Park for your picnic."

"Danny! Danny! Dad! Look! Not only did we get pizza, I got to make the pizza!"

"Wow, Mimi! Good job! That looks absolutely amazing," said her dad. "Cheers to a great day, a great city and to the perfect pizza made by Mimi herself!"

"Cheers!"

Uncle Joe's New York Style Pizza

1 Cup All Purpose Flour
1 Cup Bread Flour
¾ Teaspoon Active Dry Yeast
1 Full Recipe of Pizza Sauce
1 Cup Shredded Mozzarella
(or more!)

4 Basil Leaves Chopped or Whole
1 Cup Lukewarm Water
2 Teaspoons Sugar
2 Teaspoons Salt

Yields: 1 - 15in pie, or 2 personal size pizzas

Pre-heat your oven to 500°F. A pizza stone will work best but a cookie sheet will do the trick as well if you do not have a pizza stone. Allow the stone or cookie sheet to heat up in the oven. Place your yeast, sugar, and warm water in a bowl. Mix slightly to begin to dissolve the sugar and yeast. Let sit for 5 minutes.

Once 5 minutes have passed, place your flours, salt, and oil on the yeast mixture. Mix with your hands until it forms a ball.

Knead with your hands for 3 minutes.

Place dough in a greased bowl and cover with plastic wrap or a dish towel and allow to rest for 15 minutes.

After 15 minutes has passed knead the dough again for 3 minutes.

Allow dough to again rest in a greased bowl covered by a dish towel for 30 minutes.

Divide into two balls and start rolling out your dough! For traditional NY style pizza, you want to get a thin dough with a small lip around the edges to create the perfect crust. Do this on a piece of parchment paper (this will make it easier to transfer onto your hot pizza stone). Top your pizza to your liking!

Once your pizza is topped and ready to go, pull your oven rack with your stone 3/4 of the way out of the oven. Use the parchment paper to lift the pizza up and onto your stone. Leave the paper under the pizza, if you try to remove it, you risk messing up your perfect pizza!

Bake for 8-10 minutes at 500°F. Allow to cool and enjoy!!

Gluten Free Pizza Dough

2 Medium Potatoes
⅓ Cup Warm Water
3 Teaspoons Granulated Sugar
¼ Ounce Dry Active Yeast
1 Cup Rice Flour

½ Cup Tapioca Starch
1 Egg White
1 ½ Tablespoons Extra Virgin Olive Oil
1 Teaspoon Salt

Yields: 2 personal 10in pizzas

Pre-heat oven to 450°F. Place pizza stone or a cookie sheet in the oven. Peel both potatoes. Boil until fully cooked. Cool down in ice water. Once fully cooled, shred the potatoes on a cheese grater. Set aside.

Combine the yeast, sugar, and warm water in a bowl. Set aside and let rest for 5 minutes.

Combine the potatoes, rice flour, tapioca starch, and salt together until crumbly.

Add the egg white and oil to the flour mixture.

Add yeast mixture to the flour mixture and mix until combined.

Place dough in a greased bowl and cover with a dish towel for an hour and a half in a warm environment.

Divide into two balls.

On a piece of parchment paper, prepare your dough into the desired shape. Use a mixture of the tapioca starch and rice flour to flour the surface of the parchment paper and to prevent your hands from sticking to the dough.

Top with desired toppings and bake for 10 minutes.

Don't Forget... your pizza can be however you like it to be! Some like more sauce, some like more cheese! Some like pepperoni, some like sausage! Experiment with your toppings to make it your own!

Mimi's Fresh Pizza Sauce

4 Small-Medium Vine Tomatoes
1 Large Garlic Clove
½ Teaspoon Salt
½ Teaspoon Pepper

4 Leaves of Fresh Basil
4 Leaves of Fresh Oregano
2 Tablespoons Tomato Paste

Yields: 1 - 15in pie, or 2 personal size pizzas

Blend together in a blender or Cuisinart until smooth and fully incorporated.

ABOUT THE AUTHOR

Alyssa Gangeri is a pastry chef in New York City. She's loved baking from a young age. After graduating from The Culinary Institute of America, she traveled north and south working for companies such as The Ritz Carlton to gain knowledge and experience of the ever-growing hospitality industry. She has also competed on The Food Network's "Sweet Genius."

She developed *Mimi's Adventures in Baking* as a new way of learning for the younger generation of bakers. Her love for baking shines through in these storybook cookbooks. In her eyes, baking should be a fun experience adults and children can share together. What better way to do that than with an interactive story that makes learning your way around the kitchen exciting and easy?

When she is not making specialty cakes and pastries for her business, AllyCakesNYC, or at her restaurant, Riverwalk Bar and Grill on Roosevelt Island, you can find her in Central Park with her lively Jack Russell Terrier, Rudy, and the love of her life, Jonathan.

Mimi's Adventures in Baking New York Style Pizza is the fourth book in her baking adventure series!